WHO IS MRS GREEN ?

Copyright © 2003 by David McKee.
This paperback edition first published in 2005 by Andersen Press Ltd.
The rights of David McKee to be identified as the author and illustrator of this work
have been asserted by him in accordance with the Copyright, Designs and Patents Act, 1988.
First published in Great Britain in 2003 by Andersen Press Ltd., 20 Vauxhall Bridge Road, London SW1V 2SA.
Published in Australia by Random House Australia Pty., 20 Alfred Street, Milsons Point, Sydney, NSW 2061.
All rights reserved. Colour separated in Switzerland by Photolitho AG, Zürich.
Printed and bound in Italy by Grafiche AZ, Verona.

10   9   8   7   6   5   4   3   2   1

British Library Cataloguing in Publication Data available.

ISBN 1 84270 429 X

This book has been printed on acid-free paper

WHO IS MRS GREEN ?

DAVID McKEE

Andersen Press
London

"Jennifer, you're driving me crazy. shouted Mum.
"Go and play with Henry."

"Mum's cross with me," said Jennifer.
"It's Mrs Green's fault," said Henry.
"Who is Mrs Green?" asked Jennifer.

"Your mum's not cross with *you*, she's cross
because when she was carefully parking,
Mr Moon in the car behind, honked his horn
at her."

"Oh!" said Jennifer. "Tell me about Mrs Green."

"But," said Henry, "Mr Moon wasn't angry at your *mum*. He was annoyed because Mrs Moon had called him 'Stupid'."

"And Mrs Green?" asked Jennifer.

"Mrs Moon doesn't really think her husband
is stupid," said Henry. "She was upset because
Miss Wales told her to hurry up at the supermarket
checkout."

"I want to know about Mrs Green," said Jennifer.

"You know Miss Wales is never normally so rude," Henry continued. "She was irritable because Rose, the cat, had scratched her."

"So who is Mrs *Green*?" asked Jennifer.

"Rose doesn't usually scratch," continued Henry.
"Rose was wild because Tommy chased her."

"Is this because of Mrs Green?" asked Jennifer.

"Of course," said Henry. "Tommy likes Rose.
He was in a temper because Mrs Maude
wouldn't give him his ball back."

"All because of Mrs Green?" said Jennifer.

Henry carried on. "Mrs Maude didn't mind about Tommy's ball, she was in a bad mood because somebody had thrown toast into her window box."

"But what about Mrs Green?"

"Wait," said Henry. "That somebody was Betty Lacey. She'd thrown the toast at her brother, Bruce, who had called her a rude name, only she missed him."

"Mrs Green, Mrs Green, Mrs Green!" said Jennifer.

"When Bruce said the rude name, he was thinking about Mr Williams who had pushed past him on the stairs."

"Yes, but who is Mrs GREEN?" Jennifer asked again.

"Now," said Henry, "Mr Williams, who works nights, had been woken up early and driven mad by the sound of the lady in the flat above tripping about in her high heels."

"I know, it's because of Mrs Green," sighed Jennifer.

"That lady WAS Mrs Green," smiled Henry . . .

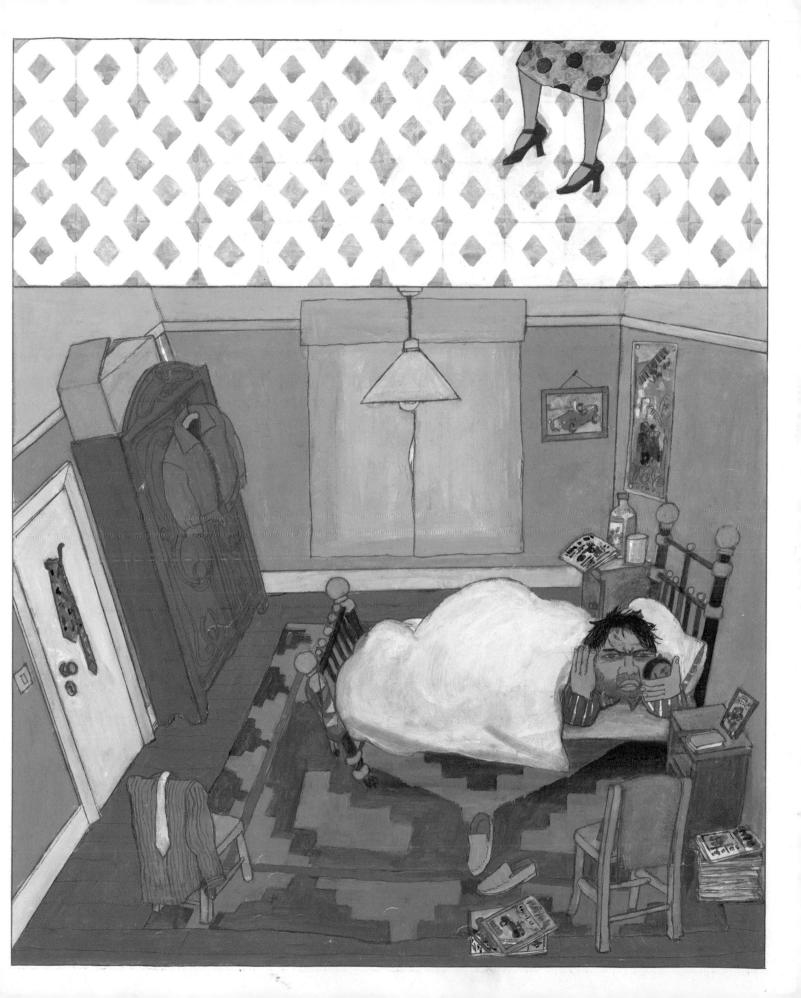

"See? Mrs Green started it. Mrs Green and her high heels!"

"Yoo hoo, Jennifer!" called Mum. "I'm sorry I was cross. Let's all sit down and have an ice-cream."
"Thanks, Mum," said Jennifer. "I know you weren't cross with *me*. It was because of Mrs Green."

"Mrs Green?" laughed Mum. "Who is Mrs Green?"

Other Andersen Press Paperback Picture Books by David McKee

The Adventures of Charmin the Bear
(illustrations by Joanna Quinn)

Charlotte's Piggy Bank

The Hill and the Rock

I Hate My Teddy Bear

The Monster and the Teddy Bear

The Mystery of the Blue Arrows

The Sad Story of Veronica Who Played the Violin

Two Can Toucan

Zebra's Hiccups

~ ~ ~

And don't miss . . .

The Conquerors
'An important book; a book we need.' Michael Morpurgo

Three Monsters

Elmer
and other titles about the popular patchwork elephant

. . . from the same artist!